Anonymous

The Arguments of Several of the Satires of Juvenal

SALZWASSER
VERLAG

Anonymous

The Arguments of Several of the Satires of Juvenal

Reprint of the original.

1st Edition 2023 | ISBN: 978-3-37514-358-9

Verlag (Publisher): Salzwasser Verlag GmbH, Zeilweg 44, 60439 Frankfurt, Deutschland
Vertretungsberechtigt (Authorized to represent): E. Roepke, Zeilweg 44, 60439 Frankfurt, Deutschland
Druck (Print): Books on Demand GmbH, In de Tarpen 42, 22848 Norderstedt, Deutschland

THE

ARGUMENTS OF SEVERAL

OF THE

SATIRES OF JUVENAL.

THE

ARGUMENTS OF SEVERAL

OF THE

SATIRES OF JUVENAL.

PREPARED FOR THE STUDENTS

IN THE

UNIVERSITY OF PENNSYLVANIA.

———————◄•●•►———————

PHILADELPHIA:

L. R. BAILEY, PRINTER, 26 NORTH FIFTH ST.

1858.

ADVERTISEMENT.

A STUDENT can but poorly appreciate one of Juvenal's Satires, till the second or third reading; and his first attempt must be especially tiresome, if, without knowing the author's drift, he is compelled to labour over some passage of difficult interpretation, with little or no help from notes, and with only two or three hours a week to spend upon it. I have sometimes endeavoured to remedy this difficulty, by pointing out the general meaning of the author, and explaining obscure passages beforehand; but this takes time, which might be more profitably spent in other ways, while it is of but little use to the student, who, not having time for reflection at the moment, cannot fully understand the explanation, and can hardly note down what he does not understand, or fix it in his memory, to reflect upon afterwards.

My reason for preparing the following arguments of the Satires commonly read, was simply to relieve, as far as possible, the difficulty I have just spoken of. The student can read them at his leisure, and thus know beforehand what his author is writing about: if he meets with a difficult passage, the argument may throw some light upon it, or, at least, it will enable him to pass it over without losing the connexion entirely. In this way time will be saved for other and more important explanations in the lecture-room, more interest will be given to those who prepare their work carefully, and the temptation to resort to translations, and other injurious and dishonest means, may be somewhat lessened. · ·

If the interest of the student in an author, so worthy to be read and studied, is increased, or if an heretofore irksome task is made more agreeable to him, I shall be fully repaid for any trouble that the work has given me. The parallel passages, noted at the foot of each page, may be of use, though without comment : no doubt many more could be found.

F. A. J.

Philadelphia, May 18, 1858.

☞ When a sentence seems to be explanatory of what precedes it, the arrangement of the poem is sometimes changed in the argument, the key-passage, (so to call it,) being printed first. In such cases it is always in italics, and the number of the line follows in parenthesis.

⁎ Passages enclosed in brackets [　], are omitted in Leverett's edition.

SATIRE I.

PROBABLY written about A. D. 100, as a preface to a volume of Satires, many of which had been published before. It is, however, not merely an introduction, but contains severe rebukes upon the prevailing vices of the time.

ANALYSIS.

1. Reason for writing satire. 81. Subject, various vices, especially—94, avarice; 127, gluttony. 147. Danger of satirising.

ARGUMENT.

1. *Must I always be a listener, and never pay these poets back in their own coin? I know all their subjects by heart, for they all handle the same, and the very marble is split with their vociferations. I, too, have gone to school, and been whipped, and learned to declaim,† and I may waste paper as well as they.

19. You think me venturous, in attempting to follow the example of Lucilius: *But in the present state of corrupt morals, the difficulty is, not in writing satire, but in abstaining from it* (line 30). 22. Eunuchs marry, women exhibit in the arena, barbers vie with the nobility in wealth, slaves wear purple, and the pettifogger and informer are carried about in state. [37. Add, that you, an honest man, are pushed aside by those, who take the vilest means to secure favour.]

---

* Cf. III. 9. " Et Augusto recitantes mense poetas."

---

† Line 16. " Consilium dedimus Sullae," et cet.
Cf. X. 167. " Ut pueris placeas et declamatio fias."

45. I have entered the lists, I shall not withdraw now, for my liver burns with rage, to see the crowd of attendants around the defrauder of a prostituted ward, and a province *mourning over its empty victory, while its spoiler, with pockets full, enjoys his punishment. 51. Why write empty epics, then, while all around me are subjects for poems of another sort, *on which, though genius be wanting, indignation will write verses, such, at least, as mine or Cluvienus's* (lines 79, 80.) 55. The husband turns pander to his wife's dishonour; Nero's chariot-driver hopes for the command of a cohort, †to replace his squandered patrimony. 63. Place yourself, note-book in hand, at the corners of the streets, if you want subjects: what do you see? Here goes a noted ‡forger of wills, shamelessly carried in an open litter; here a potent matron, who poisoned her own husband, and teaches her neighbours to do the same: in fact, if you would be anybody, or possess §wealth, you must have the courage to be a villain. 77. Look within doors, you find incest and adultery.

81. This book of mine is a medley of all things from the deluge down; for never was the abundance of vices greater; avarice has free scope; gaming is full of courage, whole chests are staked at once, and thus the ‖warlike Romans fight, money their arms, a steward their armour-bearer. Surely, it is something worse than madness, to be squandering thousands, and starving your slave at the same time.

---

* Line 50.   "At tu, victrix provincia, ploras."
Cf. VIII. 120. "Quum tenues nuper Marius disciuxerit Afros."
    VIII. 94. " Sed quid damnatio confert,
                Quum Pansa eripiat quidquid tibi Natta reliquit."

---

† Line 60.   . . . . " Dum pervolat axe citato
                Flaminiam puer."
Cf. VIII. 146. " Praeter majorum cineres atque ossa volucri
                Carpento rapitur pinguis Damasippus."

---

‡ Line 67.   " Signator falso, qui se lautum atque beatum
                Exiguis tabulis et gemmâ fecerat udâ "
Cf. VIII. 142. " Solitum falsas signare tabellas."

§ For references to works of art, vid. note 1, at end of Sat. III. p. 13.

‖ Line 91. ·   " Proelia quanta illic dispensatore videbis
                Armigero," et cet.
Cf. VIII. 9.   " Effigies quo
                Tot bellatorum, si luditur alea pernox ?"
    XIV. 5.   " Parvoque eadem movet arma fritillo."

94. Did any of your ancestors spend such sums on their own gratification? The clients no longer dine with their lord, nor, yet, is a portion of his meal distributed among them, but they crowd the threshold, and scramble for the few sesterces, which the steward, in fear and anxiety lest an imposter should receive a share, distributes among them. 99. But who are these? The very Trojugenae demand their share, aye, and the Praetor and Tribune must be waited upon, according to their rank: but, "No, first come, first served," says the freedman, "I was a slave, I know, but what care I for blood or the purple? haven't I more money than any of them? and is not Pecunia our greatest deity, though she has no temple as yet?" 117. *Thus men in the highest place, count upon the sportula as an important part of their income; can you wonder, then, that the poor come in crowds, and practice all kinds of trickery, to get a double portion?

127. How beautiful is the order of daily duties! The sportula, a visit to the forum, the courts, and the triumphal statues, and then the clients, who have waited upon their REX all day, are dismissed from the porch, and, giving over their hope of a dinner, must buy their herbs and firing. He, in the meanwhile, devours alone a whole patrimony, nor permits even a parasite to recline with him; though it would be hard to find one, who could gaze on such selfish gluttony. It brings its own punishment, however; for sudden death seizes him in the bath, and the intestate old man is carried forth to burial, amid the applause of the angry fortune-hunters.

147. Posterity can add nothing to our vices, we have reached the highest point; spread your sails, then, my Muse. But whence the ability? Whence the liberty of speech? why speak of Mucius? he, indeed, pardoned Lucilius, but will Tigellinus pardon you? No, the Christian's fate will be yours, if you describe him. 158. Shall the poisoner, then, be carried on lofty couch, and no one dare to speak? Aye! close your lips as he passes; speak not, lest you be thought an accuser. Go back to ancient and harmless themes, and fear to pro-

---

* Line 95. . . . "Nunc sportula primo
Limine parva sedet, turbae rapienda togatae."

Cf. I. 132. "Vestibulis abeunt veteres lassique clientes,
Votaque deponunt quanquam longissima coenae
Spes homini."

III. 249. "Nonne vides quanto celebretur sportula fumo?
Centum convivae; sequitur sua quemque culina."

X. 46. "Defossa in loculis quos sportula fecit amicos."

voke, as Lucilius did, the anger of the conscience-stricken; reflect upon your danger before it is too late.

*Well, then, I shall speak only of the dead.

---

* Line 170. " Quorum Flaminiâ tegitur cinis atque Latinâ."
Cf. VIII. 146. "Praeter majorum cineres," *et cet.*

SATIRE III.

ONE of the most pleasing satires of all ; full of lively description and beautiful imagery, and replete with humour. Note especially the references to works of art, in lines 89, 205 and 217; and his appreciation of natural beauties, line 18. The reference to the *" molles columbae,"* line 202, contrasted with the selfishness of men, is an excellent example of Juvenal's power *in minimis.* This satire has been imitated by Dr. Johnson, in his poem, " LONDON."

ANALYSIS.

THE MISERIES OF LIFE IN ROME.

1. Nothing for the honest man to do. 58. City overrun with foreigners. 126. No hope for the poor. 190. Conflagrations, &c. 232. Noise and tumult. 368. Various dangers at night. 315. Conclusion.

ARGUMENT.

1. My friend Umbricius, the soothsayer, departs from Rome, and I am overwhelmed with grief at losing him; yet I praise his choice in selecting the delightful retreat where dwelt the Sibyl, for though lonely, it is preferable to the horrors of the crowded city, where conflagrations rage, and houses fall, and *poets in the midst of summer heats recite their lays. 10. We stop awhile at the Porta Capena, amid scenes bound to us by sacred ties, though now perverted to lowest use ; the sacred grove a Jewish begging-place, the native beauties of the fountain violated by invading art : and here Umbricius

---

* Cf. opening of Sat. I.

2

breaks forth—I must away from Rome, for no longer is there any
living here for the honourable man; my means are daily wasting
away, and, before decrepit old age overtakes me, let me depart from
my native country, and leave it to those to whom nothing is vile, nothing difficult. Let Artorius and Catulus get contracts for public
works, for burials, and sale of captives. Once they were trumpeters,
and now they give shows of their own, and for popularity, kill whom
they choose, and then return again to their trade of lowest gains.
And why should they hesitate to do any dirty work, they, whom,
Fortune, in sportive mood, has raised to highest place? 41. What
have I to do at Rome? I cannot lie or flatter, am no astrologer to
foretell a father's death to his eager heirs, nor has my art taught me
to extract poisons. I will play neither thief nor go-between, and so,
I am unworthy to be a companion ; for none but the accomplice in
crime is now a favourite. But let not all the treasures of river or
sea deprive you of sleep, or make a powerful friend fear you.

58. Worst of all, the city is wholly Greek or Syrian; and their
habits and licentiousness they have brought with them. From all
parts of Greece they come, and insinuating themselves into noblest
houses, will some day become their masters. They possess every facul-
ty, and will practice every trade : was it not a Greek who first invented
wings? 81. Shall I not flee from these? Shall I yield to those who
were brought to Rome along with prunes and figs, and forget that in
infancy I breathed the air of the Aventine, and ate the Sabine berry ?
86. Moreover, this race know how to flatter and be believed; the dis-
course, the face, the neck, and the squeaking voice of a friend, are all
extolled. [93. Their acting is perfect.] 98. A nation of comedians, the
most noted players would be nothing among them. Whether you laugh
or weep, are hot or cold, they follow your example, nay! rather go
beyond you : they have, therefore, the advantage at all times, for they
are in constant practice : no matter what the occasion, a compliment
is always ready. [109. The whole household is liable to be corrupted
by them, for they desire to know its secrets, and thus be feared.]
115. Speaking of Greeks, pass to their schools of Philosophy; was
not he a Greek, who, though a Stoic, and mature in years, turned informer, and put his pupil Barea to death? Here, then, there is no
room for a Roman; Grecian influence prevails; they never share
a friend, but with envenomed tongue they destroy us, and we are
quietly thrown overboard after years of service.

---

* Line 90. " Herculis. Antaeum," et cet.
Vid. note 1, at end of this Satire, p. 13.

126. Though, to be sure, we need not flatter ourselves that a client can perform any service now, for what is the good of the poor man's attentions, when his betters become his rivals, and the very Praetor hurries, his lictors on the run, to salute the rich, childless women, before his colleague?* The free born Roman gives the wall to a wealthy slave; [132, who spends a Tribune's pay on a brief enjoyment, while you fear even a trifling expense.] 137. Bring forward, at Rome, a witness as pious as Numa, or Nasica, or Metellus, and the first inquiry will be about his property—his slaves, his land, his table; his character last of all. Your oath is worthless, though the holiest of the gods be called to witness it; for will the gods, forsooth, waste their thunderbolts on a poor man? But poverty, too, makes man a laughing stock (lines 152, 153). 147. Garments soiled or torn, a shoe with a gaping wound, or with many a scar, to show the coarse and recent thread, excite the scorn of the vulgar. "What right hast thou to sit in the front rows of the circus? give place, I say, and let the sleek dressed sons of low born sires applaud here." This is the law, too, of the empty-headed Otho. 160. Is a son-in-law of low estate ever received into favour? is a poor man made an heir? is he even in the council of †Ediles? The worthy Romans of slender means should long ago have marched out in compact column, for 'slow rises worth by poverty depressed;' and at Rome the evil is greatest. Everything is expensive here, and we are ashamed to live in frugal simplicity, though the old Dentatus feared it not, content among the Sabellians with simple fare and plain attire. 171. There are parts of Italy, they say, where the tunic is still the only dress, until, at least, death calls for the toga of state. Even on festal days, when the play is acted on the rustic stage, the nobles and populace are clothed alike, and the white tunic is enough for the highest Edile. 180. Here we all dress beyond our means, here all live in ambitious poverty; everything, too, must be paid for even the great man's distant recognition: and then—Hear it ye Ro-

---

* Line 129. . . . "Dudum vigilantibus orbis," et cet.
Cf. XII. 98. . . . . . . "Sentire calorem
Si coepit locuples Gallita et Paccius orbi,
Legitime fixis vestitur tota tabellis
Porticus," et cet.

---

† Line 162. "Quando (pauper) in consilio est Aedilibus."
Cf. III. 179. "Sufficiunt tunicae summis Aedilibus albae."
X. 102. "Pannosus vacuis Aedilis Ulubris."

12

mans! the free born client must give presents on the birth-day, not of a son, but of a favourite slave, which he will presently sell and add to his private gains.

190. Away let us go to Praeneste, or Volsinii, or Gabii, or Tibur, for this city is only propped up; the steward plasters up the cracks, and tells us to sleep unconcerned, though the house will presently fall on our heads. Here are conflagrations: you live in a garret, and, ere you know it, the fire has reached the third story, and your neighbours below have moved their small wares and hurried away, leaving you to be burnt up along with the *gentle doves upon the roof, whom danger drives not to desert their young. 203. Some trifling furniture had Codrus, a reclining †Chiron, and a few Greek poems, the prey of Italian mice; he had nothing in fact, and yet that nothing the fire destroyed, and naked and hungry, no one offered him shelter, or a broken crust of bread; for the poor man needs no pity. 212. If the house of the rich Asturius is destroyed, the city puts on mourning, the courts are adjourned, and ere it has yet burnt out, presents of every sort—money, †statues, books, and silver, are lavished upon him, till you would guess he had fired his own house. 223. ‡For a year's rent of a dark hole, you can buy the best of houses in some country town, and there, with a spring near by, and a garden, your own property, you may live a quiet husbandman.

232. Here, too, a man grows sick with tainted food, and then want of sleep kills him; for no sleep can enter the hired lodgings, exposed to all the noise of the streets. 239. Mark the crowded corners; the rich man, it is true, is borne above our heads in safety, but, while we hasten on, the throng in front opposes us, and the crowd behind pushes us on; we are elbowed, and struck with beams, and bespattered with mud, and trod upon by heavy feet. 249. §See there the long streak of smoke from a hundred chafing-dishes, that is the way the clients dine with their lord nowadays; each brings his own kitchen, and carries off his share, piling the heavy dishes on the head of

* For several similar passages, vid. note 2, at end of this Sat., p. 14.

† Vid. note 1, at the end of this Satire, p. 13.

‡ Line 223. "Si potes avelli Circensibus."
Cf. VIII. 118. "Urbem Circo scenaeque vacantem."
X. 81. . . "Duas tantum, res anxius optat
Panem et Circenses."

§ Vid. note on I. 95, p. 7.

an unlucky slave, who fans the fire in his hurry. Amid nodding pines and threatening fir-trees he wends his way; but presently a wagon, carrying Ligurian stone, breaks down, a mountain is emptied upon the crowd, and where are they? Body and soul have alike disappeared. 261. The household, meanwhile, unconcerned prepare for his return, the table, the fire, the bath, are ready, while he, alas! sits upon the bank of Styx, shrinking from the morose ferryman; and there he may sit for a hundred years, for he has naught wherewith to pay his fare.

268. But let us back to earth, and view the dangers of the night: how high the houses, from which broken crockery is thrown down upon your head, with force enough to bruise the flinty pavement! The prudent man should make his will before going out to dine, and pray that, as he returns, they may only *empty* their basins on his head. 278. Perhaps I meet a drunken brawler, who is in torture at having killed no one yet. But drunk as he is, he knows whom to attack with impunity; the scarlet cloak, the brazen lamp, and train of attendants, are not his prey, but me he stops, and insults, and threatens, and whether I answer or am silent, he beats me half to death, and threatens at last to have the law of me; to have a few teeth left me, is my utmost prayer. 302. Robbers, too, are abroad, for they are driven from their old haunts, and are come to Rome, where game is plenty: the most of iron is now made into chains, all the anvils are busy; the plough, the hoe, and the mattock, will soon have disappeared. O happy days of our ancestors, when one prison sufficed for Rome!

315. Other evils I might name, but the day wanes, and my muleteer beckons me: farewell, we shall meet sometimes, and I shall come armed at all points, to assist you in your war against vice.

Note 1.

I. 76.	" Argentum vetus et stantem extra pocula capram."
III. 89.	. . . . . " Cervicibus aequat Herculis Antaeum procul a tellure tenentis."
(?) III. 205.	. . . " Et recubans sub eodem marmore Chiron."
III. 217.	. . . " Aliquid praeclarum Euphranoris et Polycleti."
VIII. 3.	. . . " Et stantes in curribus Aemilianos."
VIII. 102.	" Et cum Parrhasii tabulis signisque Myronis, Phidiacum vivebat ebur; necnon Polycleti Multus ubique labor; rara sine Mentore mensa."

14

NOTE 2.

III. 202.   "(Your fellow men will hurry away and leave you to
be burnt up, who are next the roof) *molles ubi
reddunt ova columbae.*"

X. 232.   " (The wretched old man, fed by others' hands, and
gaping with toothless jaws, like the young swallow) *ad quem ore volat pleno jejuna mater.*"

(?) XIV. 77.   " Vultur, jumento et canibus, crucibusque *relictis,*
Ad fetus *properat* partemque cadaveris affert."

XIV. 254.   . . . . . " Eme quod Mithridates
Composuit, si vis *aliam decerpere ficum
Atque alias tractare rosas.*"

SATIRE VIII.

I⊤ would be impossible, in a mere outline, to do even partial justice to this noble satire. The subject is one which Juvenal was admirably qualified to handle. He was thoroughly imbued with an admiration for the stern and lofty morality of the ancient Romans; and, as he contrasted it with the dissolute and servile spirit of his own time, his mind must have swelled with honest indignation, to see the degenerate sons claiming for themselves the honours of their ancestors. There is no declamation here, " no commonplaces;" he speaks from an overflowing heart, or rather, as he says himself, with something like Divine inspiration,—" *Credite me vobis folium recitare Sibyllae.*" This Satire presents many difficulties, and must be read and studied with great care to be appreciated.

ARGUMENT.

1. Why point to the table of genealogies? why to the portraits and statues of your ancestors, these *standing in their chariots, these mutilated with age? What can they do for you? what will you gain by boasting of a Corvinus in your capacious tree, or a Master of Horse or Dictator, now smoky with age? What of all these, if before their faces the †midnight dice delight you; if, when they would lead out their armies to battle, you betake yourself to sleep, worn out with nightly revelling? 13. What right has a degenerate Fabius to

---

* Line 3. Vid. note 1, at end of Satire III., p. 13.

---

† Line 10. "Si luditur alea." Vid. note on l. 91, p. 6.

pride himself on the founders of his family, if avaricious, silly, lamb-
hearted, or effeminate; or, if a poisoner, he bring his house to *mourning? 20. The only nobility is virtue; be a Paullus in character,
place this before all ancestral busts, let this precede the Fasces even,
if you are Consul. 24. Possess excellencies of soul, and I recognise
the nobleman at once. Hail! thou, who art worthy to be a descendant of noble blood; an unwonted gift art thou to thy rejoicing
country; well may the people cry εὑρήκαμεν! συγχαίρωμεν!! 30. For
shall he be called high-born who is unworthy of his race? Sometimes, 'tis true, we name a pet dwarf Atlas, an Aethiop a swan, a
deformed girl Europa, and lean and sluggish dogs after all the most
ferocious beasts of the forest; beware, then, lest thus in derision thou
art called a Creticus or Camerinus.

39. To you, Rubellius, is my admonition addressed. You are
swollen with pride at being the descendant of the great Julius, rather
than of †humble parents, as if you had made yourself noble. " Low
born wretches," you say, " who cannot tell your father's birthplace!
I am a Cecropian." I wish you joy of your descent, and yet, from
lowest ranks the high-born man of no learning must seek for one, to
solve the knotty problems of the law: from lowest ranks a ‡warrior
springs, while you are only a Cecropian, as useless as a Hermes,
though your head, to be sure, has life in it. 56. Tell me, O descendant of Teucer, do we not praise the horse, who, in the crowded circus,

* Line 16. . . . . " Emptorque veneni,
                   Frangendâ miseram funestat imagine gentem."
" In the hall of the Grand Council at Venice, are the portraits
of the doges arranged in order of time; but in the place which ap-
pertains to the picture of Falieri, is a representation of the Ducal
throne with a black veil over it, with this inscription:—Questo è il
sito di Marino Falier, decapitato pe' suoi delitti."—Rose's Biog. Dic.
There is a somewhat different account of the same in the notes to
Byron's " Marino Faliero."

† Line 43.   " Ventoso sub aggere."
Cf. XIV. 58.   " Ventosa cucurbita,"

‡ Line 51.   " Juvenis"= a man of military age.
Cf. XIV. 7.   " Nec melius de se cuiquam sperare propinquo
                 Concedet juvenis."
             " Hic petit Euphratem."
Cf. VIII. 170. " Maturus bello, Armeniae Syriaeque tuendis
                 Amnibus et Rheno atque Istro."
' Rivers,' because they would form the proper line of military ope-
rations, especially in defence?

wins applause for speed; while the progeny of noted steeds are set
for sale, unless they often win the victory? What do we care for the
shades of their ancestors? Let them go for a small sum, and drag
carts, and turn the mill of some one. 68. Do something, then, for us
to inscribe on your own tablet; something besides the honours we
have already and willingly given to those on whom you depend.
71. Enough for him, who, devoid of common sense (a rare gift),
prides himself on his relationship to Nero. Do not thou, Ponticus
be willing to be estimated by the praises of thy ancestors alone. To
rest upon the fame of others is like a roof supported by columns,
which may fall, or the vine clinging to the elm for support. 79. In
all the relations of life be faithful; let no threats lead you to perjury;
prefer not life to honour, for which alone it is worth while to live: it
is not in eating and anointing oneself with perfumes that life consists.

87. When a province receives thee as its governor, restrain thy
passions; look with pity on our plundered allies (so we call them;)
consider, too, that rewards await the upright ruler, that the Senate
has justly punished Capito and Numitor, the pirates even of the Cili-
cians. Yet the *Province gains little by the condemnation, for the
next ruler will take what the last has left, and so, Chaerippus, you had
better sell your rags, and live as you can on the pittance they
bring you, and be not mad enough to waste your fare to Rome.
98. Just conquered, our allies suffered not as now: still much was
left them; much that was rich, and costly, and †beautiful; and
thence was fed the sacrilege of Dolabella, of Antony and of
Verres, and thence arose the spoils and triumphs of peace. 108.
Now they have but little left, and that little will be taken with vio-
lence away; even the Lares must go, if there is a god worth look-
ing at, if any of more than usual beauty in the niche. Such spoils as
these in place of greater ones, for these are the best they can get.
Some, perhaps, thou wilt despise as unwarlike, as effeminate; for
what hast thou to fear from these? but do not thus in Spain or Gaul,
nor in ‡Africa, which supplies our corn. Do not wrong the brave, for
though their money is taken, they have their arms still,

---

* Line 94. "Sed quid damnatio confert."
Vid. note on I. 50, p. 6.

---

† Line 103. Vid. note 1, at end of Satire III., p. 13.

---

‡ Line 118. "Circo scenaeque vacantem."
Vid. note on III. 223, p. 12.
Line 120. "Marius discinxerit Afros." Vid. note on I. 50, p. 6.
3

125. Call not this a common-place; a leaf of the Sibyl rather. If thy attendants are honest, if no favourite sells justice, if no wife plays the Harpy in every district, then, indeed, mayest thou trace thy lineage to the Golden age, or name the whole Titan tribe and Prometheus himself among thy ancestors. But if intrigue, and lust, and cruelty, drive thee on, and thou delight to see the lictors weary and the axes dulled with use, then thy noble ancestors will array themselves against thee and hold a torch to reveal thy degeneracy. 141. Why boast thyself to me, if in the temple, thy grandfather built, and before thy father's statue thou art a *forger; or, to hide thy head, wearest the Santonic hood?

146. †By the ashes of his fathers, Damasippus drives his chariot, and he, the Roman Consul! is not ashamed to apply the drag-chain—At night, ' tis true, but has not the night its own witnesses? When his term of office is over, he will do the same by day, nor feel a moment's anxiety at meeting and saluting with driver's token a grey-haired friend. He will act the groom, too; and, though in his sacred character, he sacrifices at the high altar of Jupiter, he will swear only by the mule-drivers' goddess. Presently he visits the midnight eating-houses and is greeted by a Syrophœnician host as " Master" and " King," and pays his bustling hostess dearly for a flagon of wine.

163. " We did the same in our youth" you will say ; true, but not as age advanced did we cherish the fault. There are crimes, which at earliest manhood should be laid aside ; but Damasippus to places of depraved enjoyment goes, when ripe for war, a defender of Nero's ‡boundaries. Danger threatens the borders of the empire ! Despatch your armies to Ostia, O Cæsar !! Send quickly !! But where is your lieutenant ? There he is ! behold him in some drinking house, with thieves, and cut-throats, and men of lowest trade, and where a Gallus lies drunk by his silent drum : there where equal liberty prevails. Should not thy slave, found thus, be sent to the §Tuscan prison ; but ye pardon yourselves, O descendants of Trojans. Brutus may do what would disgrace a cobbler.

---

* Line 142. " Falsas signare tabellas." Vid. note on I. 67, p. 6.

† Line 146. Vid. notes on I. 60, p. 6, and on I. 171, p. 8.

‡ Line 171. Vid. note on VIII. 51, p. 16.

§ Line 180. " In Lucanos aut Tusca ergastula mittas."
Cf. XIV. 29. " Quid suadet juveni laetus stridore catenae,
　　　Quem mire afficiunt inscripta ergastula, carcer
　　　Rusticus."

183. Bad though it is, there's worse to come; his money gone
Damasippus goes upon the stage to play in farces; and Lentulus,
worthy of a real cross, acts the robber Laureolus. But the People are
not innocent, for they sit and see these buffooneries of the Patricians.
192. Gladiators, too, they must be and sell their lives to the *Praetor.
Ask not for how much: what matter? no Nero compels them, and
they hesitate not to do it: but, if they were compelled, should they
not prefer death to such ignominy as this. But can you wonder at the
Nobility on the stage, when the Emperor is musician? What can
you expect but shows? This disgrace, too, the City has—that a
Gracchus, disdaining to conceal his face in the arms of a mirmillo,
fights as a retiarius. 205. His countenance is not cast down with
shame, as he flies across the arena; and his tunic and cap-strings,
too, prove that he is the priest. Worse than any wounds must it be,
to fight with such a one.

211. Would not a free people have preferred †Seneca to Nero? who,
far worse than Orestes, with no authority from the gods, with no
provocation, murdered, mother; wife, and sister, sang upon the stage,
and wrote a Trojan War! What worse than this, for what more
degrading, in all his tyranny? Such are the deeds of a high-born
prince. Let the statues of your ancestors have the honours you have
won; hang up before them your dresses, masks, and harp.

251. What more illustrious Catiline than your birth? yet you
would have destroyed the city, as though born of Barbarians. But
a Consul, of no ancestry, and of low esteem at Rome, crushed your
designs, and so bore off more glory within the city walls, than Octa-
vius from the blood-stained battle field. And Rome was free when
she called Cicero, the father of his Country.

245. Another one from Arpinum, wont to labour there for hire,
and suffer indignities as a common soldier, yet sustained the charge

---

* Line 194. " Praetoris ludis."

Cf. X. 36. "Quid si vidisset Praetorem curribus altis
Exstantem, et medio sublimem in pulvere Circi ?"

XIV. 256. . . . . "Cui nulla theatra,
Nulla aequare queas Praetoris pulpita lauti."

---

† Line 212. " Ut dubitet Senecam praeferre Neroni."

Cf. X. 15. . . . . . "Jussuque Neronis
Longinum et magnos Senecae praedivitis hortos
Clausit . . . . .
Tota cohors."

of the Cimbri, bearing destruction to the City: and after the battle was over, and the crows were wondering at the huge corpses, his noble-born colleague received only the second laurels.*

254. The souls of the †Decii, as well as their names, were plebeians, but, when the powers of Hades demanded the whole ' ROMAN PEOPLE, THE ALLIES AND THE LATIN NAME,' the soul of a Decius was ransom enough for all. 259. The last good king was of servile birth; it was the sons of the Consul, who, caring not to enroll their names among Rome's heroes, would open the gates to the banished Tarquins; and it was a slave, who revealed their plot; he, indeed, should take his place with Brutus; while they paid the just penalty of their crimes.

269. Better that Thersites should be thy father, if thou couldst wield the arms of Achilles; than that Achilles should beget thee, no better than Thersites. But go not back too far, lest from the asylum of Romulus thou draw thy descent, where congregated those I would not wish to name.

---

* Line 245. " Arpinas alius . . .
Hic tamen et Cimbros et summa pericula rerum
Excipit, et solus trepidantem protegit urbem ;
Atque ideo . . .
Nobilis ornatur lauro collega secundâ."

Cf. X. 278. . . . . " Quid illo cive tulisset
Natura in terris, quid Roma beatius unquam
Si circumducto captivorum agmine et omni
Bellorum pompâ animam exhalasset opimam,
Quum de Teutonico vellet descendere curru ?"

---

† Line 254. " Plebeiae Deciorum animae," et cet.

Cf. XIV. " Quantus erat (amor) patriae Deciorum in pectore.

SATIRE X.

One of the most powerfully written, and most sys-
tematically arrangèd, of Juvenal's Satires. Imitated
by Dr. Johnson in his poem, "The Vanity of Hu-
man Wishes."

ANALYSIS.

THE VANITY OF HUMAN WISHES.

1. Wealth, 1.—II. Power, 56.—III. Eloquence,
114.—IV. Military glory, 133.—V. Long life, 188.—
VI. Beauty, 289.—VII. Conclusion, 346.

ARGUMENT.

1. In all the world how few are found who know what is good for
them. For what are our fears or desires? What do you undertake
without repenting of it afterwards? The gods have often overturned
whole families in answer to their own prayers, *for men think it a
pious thing, to pray for what is worthless or pernicious* (line 54). 8.
And this is true both in peace and war; whether mental gifts, or
strength of arm is asked, it is all the same. But more are destroyed
by an inordinate thirst for money: *and yet riches is the principal
thing prayed for; let our wealth increase, let our fortune exceed all
others'* (lines 23, 24). 15. And what follows? By command of Nero
a whole cohort blockaded the rich man's house,* while he who sups in
a garret is safe enough. Even a small treasure carried at night
destroys a man's peace, every shadow frights him: while the empty

---

* Line 16. "Magnos Senecae praedivitis hortos," *et cet.*
Vid. note VIII. 212, p. 19. ·

traveller sings in the robber's face: poisons too are mixed in the jewelled cup, never in earthenware. 28. Is it any wonder, that Democritus laughed at all the follies of men, and Heraclitus wept over them? (The only wonder is, where he got tears enough.) As it was, the Thracian's sides were forever shaking; but what, if he were living now and should see the sumptuous trappings of our time? The procession of the Praetor,* at the 'Ludi Circenses,' rivalling the Consular triumphs of former days, even to the slave riding with him in his chariot, though not, as of old, to remind him that he is a man. He must have a sceptre too, and a train of attendants, and free born Romans at his bridle, a mercenary throng.† As it was, Democritus found matter enough for laughter, and he was no block-head, though born in the country of wethers.

56. Power is no safer than wealth, it brings envy, and destruction presently follows. A man is overwhelmed by his own honours, his image is pulled down, the very chariot and horses are broken in pieces, and the triumphal statue of Sejanus, once an object of ado-ration, is melted into the meanest utensils. See how the populace enjoy the great man's fall; hear their rejoicings, and the vituperations they heap upon him, now that he has fallen under the displeasure of the Emperor. No matter about the accusation, or the informer, or the witness; Tiberius decreed his death, and the mob follows Fortune, and would do so, if it had all gone the other way; for since they have lost the privilege of selling their votes, they have thrown care overboard, their belly and the public games are now their sole concern.‡ 81. But they are careful of themselves; "Many will perish," says one, "No doubt of it," says another, "he may melt us all up, and we may pay the penalty of lukewarmness in his cause, let's prove our loyalty by in-sulting the dead body of Sejanus; but a slave must be by as a witness, or it may all go for nothing." 88. This is the way Sejanus was treated; would you wish to be like him? to have authority and influence on such conditions? "Nay" you say, "this kind of power is a good thing; it is well to have it even though you would not use it." But, is it worth all the evils that go with it? Is not the ragged Edile§ in

---

* Line 36. "Praetorem curribus altis," et cet.
· Vid. note VIII. 194, p. 19.

† Line 46. "Quos sportula fecit amicos." Vid. note, I., 95, p. 7.

‡ Line 81. "Panem et Circenses." Vid. note, III. 223, p. 12.

§ Line 102. "Pannosus Aedilis." Vid. note, III. 162, p. 11.

some country town better off than Sejanus? Confess, then, that his was not a wise ambition, that, in aiming at excessive power, he was preparing a greater fall for himself. So it was with Crassus, and Pompey, and Cæsar, the gods were so malignant as to grant their prayers; and so it happens, that few kings die a natural death.

114. The fame of Eloquence others long for; the schoolboy would be a Demosthenes or Cicero, and even a pennyworth of schooling excites his ambition: and yet eloquence was their death; better had Cicero written bad verses, such as, "*O fortunatam &c.*" than his godlike Philippics; and it was an unlucky day for Demosthenes, when he left the anvil to learn oratory.

133. Others again the glory of war arouses to action, the spoils of battle is their aim, for these they endure toil and danger: fame, not valour, leads them on, for valour is worthless, if no reward attends it. And so they will overturn their country for their own glory, and for the sake of a memorial tablet upon their tomb, which, after all, the root of the sterile fig tree may shake to pieces. 147. Weigh Hannibal, how much is left of him now? Yet once the vast extent of Africa could not hold him, Spain did not satisfy him, he leaped over the Pyrenees, and in vain did nature oppose the snow clad Alps, their rocky cliffs he divided and burst through the mountain barrier; Italy was in his grasp, but he must break down the gates of Rome and set up the Punic Standard in her crowded streets. What a picture was the one eyed chief riding over the marshes on his elephant! and all for empty glory, for he was beaten, of course, in his turn, and presently became an exile, waiting upon the slumbers of a Bithynian tyrant: and at last he perished, not like a soldier on the battle field, but by an insignificant ring, the avenger of Cannae.* 168. For Alexander† the whole world was not enough: he fretted as one confined within a narrow island: yet at Babylon a coffin sufficed him. What wonders we believe of Xerxes

---

* Line 167.   " Et declamatio fias." Vid. note, I. 16, p. 5.

† Line 168.   "Unus Pellaeo juveni non sufficit orbis:
                Aestut infelix angusto limite mundi,
                Ut Gyari clausus scopulis parvâque Seripho."

Cf. XIV. 313.   "Sensit Alexander, testâ quum vidit in illâ,
                Magnum habitatorem, quanto felicior hic qui
                Nil cuperet qnam qui totum sibi posceret orbem,
                Passurum gestis aequanda pericula rebus."

(If indeed the lying Greeks are to be credited):* a canal through Athos, the sea bridged, rivers drunk up, and whatever else the moist-winged poet sung, the winds scourged, Neptune bound with fetters, (how merciful not to have branded him too: any of the gods would serve so kind a master). But how did he get back from Salamis? In a skiff, which through seas choked with corpses with difficulty made its way. Such are the penalties for glory paid.

188. "Give length of days,‡ O Jupiter," is another prayer, whether in health or sickness, they desire the same, forgetful of the ills that old age attend; the deformed countenance, the skin wrinkled like the hide of a mother ape, so, that whatever the differences among the young, the old look all alike; the voice and the limbs trembling, the head bald, the nose moist with second infancy, the gums toothless; and in fine he is so hateful to all, that even the fortune hunter loathes him. No taste, no hearing; the best of minstrels is unheeded, the concert of horns and trumpets is scarcely heard, the slave must shout the hour or the name of the coming guest, at the top of his voice. Besides this, his body is only warmed by fever, and an army of diseases dance around him, so many, that few things are harder to number. Weak, blind, helpless, like the young swallow which is fed by its fasting parent.‡ 232. But this is nothing to the loss of mind, for see! he does not know his slaves, nor his friends, nor his children, but, by a savage will, excludes them all and leaves his possessions to some worthless one. 240. Though the mind fail not, he lives to bury all that are dear to him: these are the penalties of the long

---

* Line 174. . . . . . "Et quidquid Graecia mendax
　　　　　　　　　Audet in historiâ."
Cf. X. 246. " Magno si quidquam credis Homero."
　III. 60. . . . . . "Non possum ferre, Quirites,
　　　　　　　　Graecam urbem," *et seq., especially*—
line 85. " Quid, quod adulandi gens prudentissima laudat
　　　　　　Sermonem indocti, . . .
　　　　　　Haec eadem licet et nobis laudare; sed illis
　　　　　　Creditur "
XIV. 229. . . . . . . "Quantum
　　　　　　Diloxit Thebas, si Graecia vera, Menoeceus," *et cet.*

---

† Line 188. " Da spatium vitae, multos da Juppiter annos."
Cf. X. 357. " Fortem posce animum, mortis terrore carentem,
　　　　　　Qui spatium vitae extremum inter munera ponat
　　　　　　Naturae."

---

　　　232. " Mater jejuna." Vid. note 2, at end of Sat. III., p. 14.

lived, to be in constant grief, and to grow old in perpetual mourning. 246. Fortunate, forsooth, was Nestor, in putting off death till past his hundredth year :* but listen, how he complains of his cruel fate, while the manly Antilochus is burned on the funeral pyre. "Why have I lived to these times, what is my crime, that I deserve such a punishment ?" So Peleus mourned Achilles, so Laertes the sea-tost Ulysses. And Priam, if he had died before Paris built his fleet, might have been gathered to his fathers, his sons carrying him to burial, his daughters giving the note of lamentation to the Trojan women. But he lived long, and saw his kingdom overthrown, and a tottering soldier, was sacrificed before the altar of Jupiter. But he was better off than Hecuba, for she lived to be transformed into a dog, he died still a man. 273. But passing Mithridates and Croesus, look at Marius, exiled, imprisoned, a beggar ; who had been happier than he, if he had breathed his last as he descended from his triumphal chariot ?† The prayers of many cities prevailed over the Campanian fever, and Pompey's life was spared, that he might lose an army and his head; while Lentulus, Cethegus, and Catiline fell unmangled.

289. Mothers will pray for beauty for their children. Why should they not? Ask Lucretia and Virginia. Anxious, moreover, must ever be the parent of a handsome boy ; for seldom are beauty and chastity united. Train him as carefully as you please, you will hardly save him ; for though he be pure and modest, he may fall a victim to the lust and revenge of others. Remember Silius and the Empress Messalina.

346. Shall we pray for nothing, then ? Better to leave it to the gods, to give us what we need; and they will bestow what is best, rather than what is pleasant. We are blinded with passion, and ask for wife and children, but only the gods can tell, what the wife and children will be. Be content, then, and if you must pray and offer vows, demand health of body and mind, a stout heart, which fears not death, which shrinks from no toil, controls its desires, and would rather endure the labours of Hercules, than live in lust and effeminacy. These things we can get for ourselves, we need not supplicate Fortune, for she has no power over us, if we are prudent.

---

* Line 246. "Rex Pylius, magno si quidquam credis Homero,
          Exemplum vitae fuit a cornice secundae," et cet.
Cf. XII. 128. "Vivat Pacuvius, quaeso, vel Nestora totum."

† Line 282. "Quum de Teutonico, vellet descendere curru."
Vid. note on VIII. 245, p. 20.

4

SATIRE XII.

Contains some pleasantry, but not much satire, except the reference, towards the last, to the legacy-hunters.

ARGUMENT.

1. More pleasant than my natal day is this, Corvinus. Votive sacrifices I offer to the gods; a lamb to Juno, an equal offering to Minerva, and a wanton bull, just weaned from his mother, to Jove. He shakes his rope, and tosses his head, and pushes against the oak-tree with his horns. If my means were equal to my love, a bull, fat with the pasture of the Clitumnus, should honour the return of my Catullus, scarce yet recovered from the terrors of the sea, and wondering at his safety. 17. For not only the dangers of the deep, but the lightning he has escaped. The bolt descended upon the shrouds, and such a storm, as poets write of, arose in fact. *And now another misfortune, though not a new one, as every votive tablet proves, happened to our Catullus : for know, as the crazy ship staggered in the waves, and the skill of the master brought no help, they began to bargain with the winds by throwing their treasures overboard. Even the garments, made of wool which the rich grass or the hidden virtues of the fountain and Baetic air had coloured; cups of silver, too, from which the Macedonian had drunk. Who else in these degenerate days would dare to prefer life to silver. Still the vessel does not

---

* Line 26.   . . . "Pars dira quidem sed cognita multis,
Et quam votivâ testantur fana tabellâ
Plurima. Pictores quis nescit ab Iside pasci."

Cf. XIV. 300. " Frigida sufficient velantes inguina panni
Exiguusque cibus, mersâ rate, naufragus assem
Dum rogat et pictâ se tempestate tuetur."

right till at last the mast is cut away. 57. *Wilt thou go to sea now, and trust thy life to a log ? take, then, a basket of bread, and a big flagon, and see, too, that you have a hatchet in case of storms.

62. After a while the sea fell calm, and with better fates the ship went on with clothes spread out, and one sail at the prow. Now the sun brightens and hope revives, the Alban peak is seen, and the harbour of Ostia entered : the master seeks the inner basin with his broken vessel, and there they land, and love to tell their dangers. 83. Go, boys, and with reverent lips and hearts prepare for a sacrifice. Presently I shall come, and, that duty performed, I shall return and crown my Lares : the boughs are at the door, and morning lamps hang over it.

93. Suspect me not, Corvinus; †Catullus has three little heirs : for such a one's recovery, a legacy-hunter would not offer a dying hen, much less a cock to Aesculapius. Let the rich Gallita or Paccius fall sick, and votive tablets will hang in all the portico ; nay! men will start up and offer a hundred bulls, for elephants are not for sale in these parts ; they are brought from afar, and kept as Caesar's herd ; as of old they obeyed Hannibal and Pyrrhus. 111. But Novius and Pacuvius would offer them if they could, to the Lares of Gallita. One of them, indeed, would sacrifice his finest slaves; or, if he had a daughter at home like Iphigenia, she should be given to the altar, though he could expect no miracle to save her. 121. Bravo! my fellow citizen ; surely the thousand ships of the Greeks are not to be compared to the will of a rich man ; and, if he recovers, he must, no doubt, destroy his former will, and leave all in a few words to Pacuvius. See, then, how much he gains by slaying his daughter.

127. Long live Pacuvius, then, even a whole Nestor ; let Nero's wealth be his, whole mountains of gold; and never let him love, or ever be beloved.

---

* Line 58.   " I nunc et ventis animam committe dolato
          Confisus ligno, digitis a morte remotus
          Quatuor aut septem, si sit latissima taeda."

Cf. XIV. 287. . . . . . "Parcat tunicis licet atque lacernis,
          Curatoris eget, qui navem mercibus implet
          Ad summum latus et tabulâ distinguitur undâ."

---

† Line 93.   " Nec suspecta," et cet. Vid. note on III. 129, p. 11.

SATIRE XIV.

The subject of this Satire is the influence of parents'
vices upon their children. It is written in a style of
great dignity as well as vigour, and contains many
admirable precepts and well chosen illustrations: one
of these is inserted in a foot-note to line 85, for the
sake of Gifford's excellent translation.

ARGUMENT.

1. Ill omened often are the examples and precepts of a parent: before the bulla is laid aside, the child has learned to brandish a little
dice-box;* and, though of soldier's years,† he gives little hope of better
things, if a hoary glutton has taught him to season the mushroom
and souse the swimming fig-pecker: at his seventh year he is passed
reform; though a thousand reverend teachers are brought to bear
upon him, never will he degenerate from the kitchen of his fathers.
15. Will the son of Rutilus be gentle and forgiving, or will he learn
from his father's example, to rave and storm at his slaves?—A father,
whose greatest joy is in the twang of scourges and the branding-irons
of the torturer, or the clanking of chains and the distant slave-prison.‡
25. What can you expect of Larga's daughter? will she be pure, who
was her mother's confidant in crime? Nay! even now she follows
in her footsteps, and uses the same go-betweens as instruments of
vice. 31. This is nature's teaching; the influence of home vices,
undermining the heart, is most powerful; for, though one or two, of
better clay, may reject it, the majority are led, or dragged along, the

---

* Line 5.   "Movet arma fritillo."   Vid. note I. 91, p. 6.

† Line 7.   "Concedet juvenis."   Vid. note VIII. 51, p. 16.

‡ Line 24.   "Carcer rusticus."   Vid. VIII. 180, p. 18.

path so constantly pointed out to them. 38. From damnable wick-
edness abstain, then, for this above all other reasons, lest our children
imitate our crimes; for ready enough are all to follow the lead of
evil, and a Catiline in every clime is found, but rarely a Brutus or
Cato.

44. Foul language away, there is a child here! Far hence, ye
strange women and filthy parasite! To a child is due the greatest
reverence; let him deter thee, if thou wouldst commit a crime, for,
though young, he will learn from thee; and then, if the Censor's
wrath should fall upon him, thou wilt doubtless chide and disinherit
him; yet thou, an old man, art worse than he: crazed and empty, is
this head of thine.*

58. If a guest is coming, spotless must be the house; the master
will rave and storm, if a filthy courtyard displease his friend, though
this a little labour would soon remedy; and shall thy son be reared
where moral pollution abounds? Look to it that he be fit for his
country's service—for the fields, for peace, for war. For he will be
a good or bad man according to the traits which thou shalt give him.
Even as the storkling, when first it takes to wing, seeks through un-
frequented wilds the reptile, for reptiles were its food when young:
and as the vulture forsakes the carrion to bear a morsel of the 'loathsome dainty' to its nestlings,† and thus rears up a carrion eating progeny; while the eagle seeks more generous prey, for fawns and hares
the parent bird had first supplied it with.‡

---

* Line 58. "Ventosa cucurbita." -
Cf. VIII. 43. "Ventoso sub aggere."

---

† Line 77. . . . . "Crucibusque relictis,
                    Ad fetus properat."
Vid. note 2, at end of Satire III., p. 14.

---

‡ Cf. Gifford's Translation:—
"The stork with newts and serpents from the wood
And pathless wild supports her callow brood;
And the fledged storklings, when to wing they take,
Seek the same reptiles through the devious brake.
The vulture snuffs from far the tainted gale,
And, hurrying where the putrid scents exhale,
From gibbets and from graves their victim tears,
And to her young the loathsome dainty bears;
Her young grown vigorous hasten from the nest
And gorge on carrion with the parent's zest,
While Jove's own eagle, bird of noble blood,
Scours the wide champaign for untainted food,

86. So it is with men: Cetronius was a builder; in one and another of the favourite haunts he reared surpassing villas, and he bequeathed to his son, at once a diminished fortune, and a still stronger passion for wasting it upon houses and marble. 96. Senseless rites are practiced, and the inhospitable laws of Moses obeyed by some; but it has come from their fathers, who idled away and lost the seventh part of their life.

108. All these vices are willingly imbibed; but avarice, too, they must learn, and that by compulsion; for they think it a virtue, it looks gloomy, and the praises of the miser are in no doubtful terms; he is frugal, he is watchful of his own, aye! and of himself too, like the serpent, that guarded the guardians of the golden apples. 114. Besides, all the people think him a great man for making money; and rightly so, but it is by doubtful means, and by constant toil. And so the father, thinking that the avaricious only are happy, exhorts his son to join that school. 124. He grounds him thoroughly in the rudiments, and then the higher branches are easily learned. First, he teaches him to pinch his slaves of their allowance; to lock up the remains of to-day's repast for to-morrow, though by to-morrow it will surely spoil, and any beggar would refuse to sit down to it.

. 135. But why this getting? why live in want, that you may die in plenty? The more you have the more you desire; a second villa is added to the one you already have; you buy your neighbour's fields; if he will sell them, and, if not, force him to do so by sending your hungry oxen to eat up his crops. "What harm does the trumpet of foul fame do me?" you say, "I don't care a bean's-shell for the praises of the whole village, if poverty is the condition." 156. Of course you escape the ills of humanity, too, and have a longer and happier life, if you possess alone more land than the whole Roman people did in earliest times; even at a later day, two jugera was enough to reward the worn-out soldier for his many wounds, who never thought this a shabby discharge of his country's promise. 116. They were fully rewarded by this trifle of land; and there in a cottage dwelt the father and his family in homely simplicity: the children, masters and slave, played together; the grown-up brothers re-

---

Bears the swift hare or swifter fawn away,
And feeds her nestlings with the generous prey:
Her nestlings, hence, when from the rock they spring
And, pinched by hunger, to the quarry wing,
Stoop only to the game they tasted first,
When clamorous, from the parent shell they burst."

turned from their work, and a second supper of porridge was smoking for them. A pleasure garden now would take more land than this. 173. Most crimes come of avarice; nothing has murdered more than the cruel lust of immoderate wealth; for he, who would be rich, must be rich quickly.

179. The Marsian and Hernician of old taught their children contentment and frugality.—" The rural deities who taught us to reject the bitter acorn, are pleased with this: the plain man desires not to commit crime; it is that purple they talk about, which leads to impious deeds." 189. How different now! The young man is aroused near midnight, though in winter, with exhortations to write, plead, study, do anything in short, which will bring money: a soldier, let him waste his life in getting a fat office, by the time he is too old to enjoy it; or a merchant, let him buy and sell, whether perfumes or hides, provided the money smells genuine: the noble precept of the poet, " UNDE HABEAS QUAERIT NEMO, SED OPORTET HABERE," should be ever on his lips: this to creeping boys is taught, this to girls before the alphabet. 211. O empty headed man! why hurry on your son? Rest in peace; he will as certainly surpass you as Ajax did Telamon: spare his tender years; a shorter way he will soon discover; he will perjure himself for gold; he will murder his newly married wife for her dower. 224. Tell me not, that you did not teach him this; you filled his mind with a love of wealth; and so you made him avaricious: you taught him to double his patrimony by fraud, and so gave him a loose rein, and it is in vain you try to stop him now, for no one is content to sin just as much as you permit him. 235. He, who tells a young man, that it is folly to aid a friend or relation teaches him to seek wealth by *every* means: wealth, your love for which is as great as that of the Decii for their country,* or of Menoeceus for Thebes, even if all the tales of the lying Greeks should be credited.† 245. You, then, lighted the spark, and you shall see the fire spreading far and wide: nay! as the lion destroyed his trainer, so shall your son destroy you: already has he gone to the astrologers; but he cannot wait their time, and if you would live till another autumn or another spring,‡ provide yourself at dinner with an antidote for poisons, which fathers as well as kings should have.

* Line 239. "Quantus erat patriae Deciorum in pectore."
Vid. note VIII. 254, p. 20.

† Line 240. "Si Graecia vera." Vid. note X. 174, p. 24.

‡ Line 253. "Si vis aliam decerpere ficum," *et cet.*
Vid. note 2, at end of Satire III., p. 14.

256. Dost thou want a strange spectacle? Go not to the *Praetor's shows: look rather at the dangers men undergo for money; which they must give to Castor to keep for them, since Mars could not save even his helmit from the robbers. 262. Mind not the festivals, men's toils are better sights than these. Can the petaurus or the rope-dancer amuse us half so much as he who lives at sea, a miserable trafficker in bags and Cretan wine? He for a slender living risks his life, you for a thousand talents. 275. Look at the harbours, filled with ships, fleets sail everywhere, if only there is a hope of gain to lead them on. Well worth your while to endure such toil; and all for but a poor return. 284. All madness is not the same, Orestes had one, Ajax another sort; and he is as certainly mad, who, for the sake of bits of stamped silver, trusts his life to a plank,† as if he raved and tore his garments. 292. "Loose the rope," he cries, "mind not this summer thunder." Unlucky wretch! this very night he must throw himself from the broken planks and swim for life, with purse in left hand and mouth. 298. And after all his extravagant desires, he will become a beggar, and gaze at himself in a painted tempest.‡

303. Gained by labour, wealth is guarded with anxiety; the buckets are in order, and a cohort of slaves must watch all night, lest the fire destroy the expensive furniture. How much better the tub of the Cynic, which burns not, and which can be patched up or replaced, if broken. Alexander felt that Diogenes was better off than himself.§ Let us be prudent, and Fortune has no power over us. 316. Dost thou ask me what is enough? Just as much as nature needs, as Epicurus and Socrates before him, had of old. Nature and Philosophy always speak alike. Or to mix something of later style, take a knight's portion, or, if that is too little, take two or three; if still not satisfied, thou art beyond hope, the wealth of Croesus or Narcissus Claudius's favourite will not suffice thee.

---

* Line 257. "Praetoris pulpita." Vid. note VIII. 194, p. 19.

† Line 289. "Ad summum latus," et cet.
Vid. note XII. 58, p. 26.

‡ Line 302. "Et pictâ se tempestate tuetur."
Vid. note XII. 27, p. 26.

§ Line 313. "Qui totum sibi posceret orbem."
Vid. note X. 168, p. 23.